NORTHWITCH
PRESS

They Dwell With Us

Vanessa Amohia Jones

NorthWitch Press

Emergence

The Early Years

One evening, too, by the nursery fire,
    We snuggled close and sat round so still,
When suddenly as the wind blew higher,
Something scratches on the window-sill.
A pinched brown face peered in—I shivered ;
No one listened or seemed to see ;
The arms of it waved and the wings of it quivered,
    Whoo—I knew it had come for me ;
  The Changeling. Charlotte Mew 1869 –1928

The Mouths of Babes

Born Uncanny

The first time my words put fear in a man's heart, I was just a baby. According to family lore, I made a real estate agent jump out of his skin.

I couldn't walk yet, but I was a preternaturally early talker. Speaking in full sentences before my first birthday I quickly developed an adult vocabulary. My family weren't phased. They watched it develop, one day, one word at a time. Had I been born in the Middle

Ages however, people would certainly have whispered words like 'changeling', 'elf-get' and 'faerie stock' behind my mother's back.

The hapless young estate agent paid no attention to me, perched on my mother's hip, while they strolled through empty rooms. No doubt he thought of young babies as barely sentient blobs. My mother plopped me down on the carpet as they continued to talk.

I listened.

Eventually there was a lull in the conversation.

"This property has a lot of trees on it." I observed.

The real estate agent spooked like a green horse.

The colour drained from his face.

He gaped at me.

"It talked!" He blustered, trying to regain his composure.

My mother always told the story with a laugh. To think, that her sick, frail child who'd barely made it into this world, had scared a grown man.

Uncanny little thing.

Made him jump right out of his skin.

Face in a Forgotten Mirror

I still dream about the old house. Sometimes the dreams are comforting, sometimes they're terrifying. Usually, I dream I'm still living there, secretly, like a ghost. Trapped, walking the endless hallways, even though it is crumbling to the ground and abandoned.

I was only a little girl when I saw the face in the mirror. It deeply unsettled me. Perhaps it shouldn't have, it was my face. Not distorted or twisted. The problem was, there was no mirror. Not anymore.

There had been a mirror, you could see that. There were strips of paint torn off the wall in a perfect rectangle above the hand-basin.

A hundred years ago the room had been a dairy cool store. It retained its original frigid quality. Somebody had painted the bathroom an eccentric midnight blue at some point.

Now, where butter had once been churned and milk set into cheese, there was an ancient toilet. The metal cistern perched six feet above the bowl with a long chain hanging for the flush. A lonely handbasin and far too much space completed the bizarre water closet.

A strange room in a house full of oddities, I wasn't afraid of it at first.

The atmosphere of dust and secrets was romantic to begin with. Victorian era newspapers wallpapered the tiny attic rooms. Excessive numbers of empty bedrooms branched out from long musty hallways.

During daylight hours the house was my kingdom. Sun drifted lazily through windows, the glass warping and thick at the bottom. I set up teddy bear picnics in the attics. I crept through holes in the wall to find old bottles in the crawl spaces. I danced like a princess on the polished floors of a palatial dining room we never used.

My own room was in the oldest part of the house where a set of French doors was barred shut. The porch they once led to was long gone, leaving a ten-foot drop and a ladder of ivy, pushing insistent tendrils through the cracks.

The garden rambled extravagantly in every direction from wide verandas. Roses, vines and trees tumbled over one another creating a jungle of imaginary kingdoms. I loved the house in the daytime.

At night it turned sinister. I had to run past the shadowy, twisting stairwell at bedtime. I'd leap from a distance into my bed to avoid the cold, grasping hands I sensed, then shiver alone, unable to sleep.

Fingers of ivy spread darkly across the wall, threatening to tangle me in their spidery grasp. Curtains of dread hung in heavy folds around my dreams. Waking from one nightmare after another, I would finally find the courage to make the dash.

Helter-skelter, lickety-split!

I pelted down miles of dark hallway. Shot past the yawning abyss of a stairwell without daring to look. Hurtled like a wet puppy into the warmth and safety of my mother's bed, where I stayed until morning light chased the ghosts away.

So long as the sun was up, I had a truce with the ghosts I'd come to believe in. Sometimes I left little gifts for them in the crawlspaces. Then one day I saw the transparent and stretched out figure of a man in brown trousers standing in the kitchen door. The summer sun shone right through him. I wasn't afraid then. I felt peaceful; entranced. But another day, I saw a formless white shape drifting down the stairs, vanishing when I blinked. The sight made me shudder. Those nasty stairs! I tried not to look at them after dark.

The bathroom in the old dairy cool store was at the base of those stairs. Cold enough to keep the butter hard, even in summer, I'd hurry in and hurry out. Maybe I'd remember to wash my hands. The tap water was icy because hot water took forever to come through miles of old pipes.

I did wash them that day. Swishing my hands briskly I glanced at the wall above the taps. My own face looked back at me from the mirror. My faded blue t-shirt, a familiar tousled mop of mousy hair and hazel eyes. We smiled at each other. I looked down to turn off the tap before I remembered.

There is no mirror.

My lungs felt suddenly empty when I looked again. There was only a dark blue, painted wall, with strips of paint torn off in a perfect rectangle. I felt sick as I ran back to my room.

Somehow it was worse than seeing them, knowing they could see me.

I look back and shiver, wondering; did the house take a little piece of my soul that day?

Perhaps that's why I continue to return in my dreams, wandering the endless hallways like a ghost.

The Corpse Candle

ong Before internet debates about whether photographed orbs are really just specks of dust or insects, our ancestors spoke of strange lights in the land. Of Corpse Candles, Willow the Wisps, Fetch lights and Jack O' Lanterns.

Long before I ever messed about with the paranormal or dabbled in the occult, I was a rebellious teenager sneaking out for a smoke. After my parents were in bed, I would crawl out my bedroom window and sit on the kitchen roof. I'd light up a Benson and Hedges and savour the heady rush of nicotine lifting me like the vast ocean swells of the west coast beach where we swam during the day.

True darkness reigns on a moonless night in the countryside. There are shades of black city dwellers never get to see. Thick. Dense. A suffocating velvet blanket pressing against your skin.

Perched on the roof, blowing out clouds of smoke, I could barely see the tea-trees outlined against the starry skyline. On more than one of those nights, I was intrigued to see a tiny blue light wending its way between the trees. It always started way down by the creek, and made its way purposefully, dodging trees and bumping over logs, all the way to the top of the hill, where it disappeared. The same pathway every time.

Not something an insect or a speck of dust would do. Besides, we don't have fireflies in Tasmania.

Don't Turn Around

We're in the middle of a coastal winter and our new house is on the edge of a swamp. Ceaseless rain, driving wind.

Thick, squelching mud invades our lawn as the wetland advances.

Yet in my dream it's summer.

Sharp, vivid, undistorted by the bent mirror of sleep, everything looks real. My new bedroom, my window with the blind half-raised. The garden outside, cradled by a tall wooden fence.

A night sky filled with stars.

In wake-time, there's nothing out there but grass, half swallowed by puddles, bounded by old trees.

In the dreamscape there's a lush vegetable garden. Full-bellied summer bounty. Corn stalks tall as a man, swollen cobs with dry silken tassels.

Motionless heat, waiting.

Then I see her. She's facing the rows of corn. Pale, bobbed hair tied back with a dusty pink ribbon. Delicate tucks on the sleeves of her ivory silk dress.

Homemade, smelling of first communion.

But it's all wrong.

The back of her dress has been brutally ripped from neck to waist. Fabric hangs in tatters, horrifyingly still in the breathless night.

Dread holds me at the window. I feel suddenly cold.

There's no blood on her, not a scratch, but I know.

The crawling sensation all over my skin tells me. Her grim stillness talks.

Run.

I struggle to tear my eyes from her.

Heavy, unwilling, my limbs will barely move.

Please don't turn around.

I wake with a thud.

Face in my pillow, breathing hard. The rain hushes steadily on the roof.

My throat is dry as summer dirt.

My brother sits on the living room floor, playing street fighter two in the dark. I have to step over his legs on the way to the kitchen.

He playfully lifts a leg as if to trip me, then drops it just in time with a goofy laugh. I force a smile then put my middle finger up at him. It's a habit.

He seems so innocent.

Blissfully unaware that something terrible once happened here, in our new house.

Close To Home

As Stephen King said, "Some shine and some don't." When eerie gifts run in the family, curious spirits are drawn like moths to a candle. The uncanny becomes commonplace, and occasionally danger comes to your doorstep.

Rocky Says Goodbye

R ocky was born in the ghetto. Before we rescued him, as a tiny kitten, he'd been squeezed too hard by toddlers and dropped on his head. He was never quite normal. What kind of cat allows little girls to push him around in a doll's pram? Or tie a bonnet on his head? Or sit him in a highchair and spoon feed him?

Rocky endured these indignities and more, without protest. He actually seemed to enjoy it. He wasn't smart and his hunting skills were zero. He left tabby and white hairs in little puddles where he slept in the sun. He was punctual for dinner time, and always ended the evening in our beds, upside down with a grin on his goofy face.

Due to his rough start in life, he had a strange wheeze. If he was curled up at your feet sleeping, you'd hear a soft rhythmic whistle in his breath. I'd wake in the night to discover he'd been hiding in my room and was now curled up on my bed. His warm weight pressed on my feet and his rusty exhales filled the darkness.

Halfway through the night he would wake me up meowing to be let out. I got in the habit of checking under my bed and in my cupboards before I went to sleep, fishing him out and plopping him down in the hallway.

One damp autumn night I performed all the checks and found no sign of Rocky. I drifted off listening to the lullaby of rain on the roof but woke again after midnight. A familiar weight was nestled against my feet. A gentle rhythmic whistle accompanied by a rumbling purr. *I wonder where the little bugger was hiding this time?*

I couldn't be bothered putting him out. Little sod. I smiled to myself. I listened to the rain and Rocky whistling while I dozed off again.

In the morning, I searched the room for Rocky. There was no sign. There was no tell-tale puddle of tabby and white hairs on the foot of my bed. The silence made my heart sick. A foreboding chill ran up my spine.

He didn't come home for dinner. He wasn't around at bedtime. It was still raining outside. It rained all week. I searched the ditches on my way to work every day. On Saturday I walked up the road in the opposite direction.

I found him then and finally brought him home. But he'd already been home, hadn't he?

To say goodbye.

Andrew

Someone brought a sack of bits and pieces from the old hospital into the museum. Lois and I were excited at first, the bag had lain forgotten in a cupboard for nearly eighty years. Perhaps it held some fascinating medical artifacts? We were disappointed when all we found were old light fittings. Half a dozen wall-mounted bedside lamps in the art deco style, a bit battered.

"Does the Museum even want these?" I asked.

"I don't know." Lois shrugged. "We can leave that decision for the committee."

We drifted back to our own tasks, Lois tapping quietly on her keyboard while I wrestled the arms of somewhat horrifying vintage mannequins into new outfits.

Hours in the museum always passed quickly. I loved that place, with its dust and old-book smell, archives spilling off the shelves, ever in need of cataloguing.

When the morning was over, I gathered my things and went to say goodbye to Lois. I was quickly swept into conversation about the old photographs she was scanning. It was fascinating, but my phone kept distracting me. Out the corner of my eye I could see random apps opening and the screen flashing. Not wanting to seem rude I shuffled it into my handbag and finished our conversation at a relaxed pace. I didn't bother about my phone again until I got home.

I still used to smoke back then.

Filthy, I know.

I rolled one and sat outside with a hot cup of tea, intending to blob on my phone for a few minutes. I hardly had it open, when the movie-making app opened itself.

Odd.

That app had only been used once, by my kids, last year when the river flooded. I was about to close it again - *must have accidentally brushed it* - when it began writing. By itself. I was transfixed. Text appeared rapidly in the caption box, with tiny clicking sounds.

"I remember that day. When it rained and rained and rained." I placed the phone hurriedly on the outdoor table, to prove to myself I wasn't touching anything.

Was the app recapping our old movie? Was that a feature? Could it be something to do with predictive text? My heartrate accelerated as the typing continued.

"I see you there, puffing on the baccy. Having your smoko time."

Not predictive text.

I never use those old-timey expressions.

I shivered. A prickling sensation I knew all too well enveloped me. A feeling that belonged in graveyards and hospitals.

Click, click, click.

"I like you. I love you."

A little shiver caressed me.

"Who is this?" I asked.

Click. Click.

"Andrew."

Holy shit! The sacred grail of the paranormal, a sentient response. And I have *zero* contacts named Andrew.

"Honey!" I hollered to my partner, indoors. I needed a witness. Of course he didn't hear me. Type continued to race across the screen.

Click, click, clickety click.

"It was when I was at school. And I was coming home..."

"Honey!" I hollered louder. He *had* to see.

Click. click. Click.

"I was sick and I huuuuuuuuuuuuuurt-tttttttt." The characters malfunctioned. A stream of jumbled letters began to appear at great speed.

Clickety, click, click, click.

My partner finally stepped outside.

"What's going on?"

"Look! Look at my phone. It's typing by itself!" He watched as a stream of nonsense appeared.

"I know it's just gobbledygook now. But look, look..." I scrolled back and showed him the conversation. "He even answered my question!"

"That's crazy!" He believed me though, beginning to catch my fevered excitement.

We watched as my phone continued to spew out random letters. The flood eventually slowed to a trickle.

"I don't think I'm going to get any more sense out of it." I sighed.

My thoughts whirred and buzzed. Someone unseen had followed me home. A ghost had used my phone. I felt like I'd witnessed a miracle.

"I think it must have been those light fittings from the old hospital." I mused. "Andrew was somehow attached."

My phone was never the same again. Every day the movie app would open by itself and ramble incoherently. Then other apps began unexpectedly popping open.

"Hey honey, my phone's doing an Andrew again." We'd both laugh.

The phone was fried, impossible to use, and finally I had to say goodbye to Andrew and get a new one.

At the time I thought nobody would ever believe a ghost had possessed an iPhone. Since then, however, paranormal experts have created a phone app specifically for chatting with the dead. Some people might be sceptical of an app like that, but I believe them.

I know.

I downloaded Andrew.

The House at the Crossroad

It was cold that year. So cold, it actually snowed. The children skipped around on the front lawn catching snowflakes and stomping footprints into the powder while they waited for the school bus. It was magical.

One night I let the girls sleep in the living room next to the hearth, since their room was frigid. In the wee hours I woke to stoke the fire. The front door stood wide open, chilly gusts of wind blasting into the house. I shut and locked it. When I turned around my youngest, five years old, stared at me with big, trembling eyes.

"I shut it three times already Mummy, but it keeps opening."

Bugger that!

I shoved a heavy tool chest up against the door and scooped her up, running down the hallway and bundling her into bed. I woke the others and helped them stumble sleepily to their bunks.

In the morning, the front door was open, the tool chest shoved a few inches across the carpet. My stomach felt sick.

I'd found the door open in the morning a few times already. I'd begun checking and double checking when I locked it. Gave it a good shake and rattle. Banged it and jiggled it. The lock was fine.

I had to face it. Too many strange things were happening in this house, the house at the crossroads.

We hadn't been there long. New farm job; new home.

A winding, treacherous road led to a small strip of houses in a settlement that used to be. The old wooden cottages had mostly been swallowed by forestry or burned down. Rows of silent trees covered their secrets, yet every spring, strips of daffodils pushed up between the trees, unaware that the house they belonged to was long gone.

At the top of the hill, another dusty metal road crossed the main track, and on one corner stood an ordinary modern brick home. Built on the site of a cottage that had burned to the ground.

I loved it there, but things were getting creepy. It wasn't just the front door.

The tiny kitchen had no room for our fridge, so it lived on the back porch. Every time I had a cup of tea, I had to go out the back door to get the milk.

To my great frustration, I'd be making a cuppa, go to get milk, and find the door locked. I blamed my children, I blamed myself. Perhaps I'd done it absent mindedly? I fiddled with it and slammed the door a few times to see if it was faulty. It wasn't.

One day, the children were at school and I was baking. By now I was being mindful not to lock that door carelessly. I popped through to get butter, then turned back to get eggs. The door was locked.

I stopped and stared. An uncanny feeling wormed around in my belly. At that moment I heard a voice, quiet as if far away.

"Tuck them in, shut them in and lock the door behind them!"

An old man. Not frightening, rather, eerie. And good advice, considering. Some of the locals were scary. But not as scary as the other things happening.

The front gates were often found open in the morning. I always shut them carefully because of the dog. Good old boy liked to wander. I thought the local boys were pranking me. Full sized metal farm gates, a length of fencing wire twisted firmly to latch them. They couldn't come undone by mistake.

It was raining heavily one morning. I could see the gates through the window, fastened properly. I dashed into the deluge to bring in extra firewood. I hurried past my car, parked out in the weather, running back with an armload of wood and dumping it on the hearth. Dusting bits of bark off my clothing, I looked out the window. The gates were wide open.

What the fuck?

I ran out immediately to shut them only to be confronted by my car, all four doors hanging wide open, rain blowing in one side and out the other.

There was nobody around. No vehicles, nobody walking. The children were cosy inside.

Things escalated.

"Were you listening to Irish music last night?" I asked my son.

"No! I thought you were listening to Irish music."

"It sounded like it was coming out of the wall."

When I *did* listen to music the speakers went crazy. The music stopped and the speakers began to buzz, like someone trying to speak, muffled by radio static. Or distorted morse code. I'd switch everything off and wait, then try again.

One night, unable to sleep, I listened to my stereo in bed. Right on midnight the interference began.

Buzz. Buzz. Buzz.

Pip. Pip. Pip.

Dot. Dot. Dash.

BANG!

The power went out.

When I flipped the circuit breaker back on, my stereo was dead.

It took us a few days to realize that every heater, the TV, the video, the stereo, the microwave and the fridge were all gone. The pump for the water tank too. The electrician had to come out for that. He showed me the scorched parts of the unit where it had sparked and sizzled. Said it must have been a huge power surge.

I phoned the power company. There was no surge.

I put charms and folk magic items around the house to ward off restless spirits, but the activity continued.

I became sick, vomiting every morning, a bunch of thick yellow stuff. I joked that it looked like ectoplasm. I was constantly nauseous and lost weight.

One of the girls dreamed that old ladies and small children were gathered on our lawn trying to get inside. My son dreamed that our dog was digging frantically by the gate, whining and barking.

Then I dreamed about a large owl perched on my windowsill. He showed me daffodils. The daffodils were important. He explained that I needed to add hot chillis to my folk charms if I wanted to banish the restless spirits wandering in from the crossroads.

I was in so deep by now, I didn't even question it. I bought some chillis the next day and hung festive looking bunches on every door and windowsill. We did a deep spiritual cleanse of the house involving frankincense and prayers to St Michael.

Finally, the activity slowed down and the ghosts stayed outside, although the tool chest remained jammed up against the front door, and occasionally, in the morning the door was open.

I researched the history of the old house. The one that burned down. My reading quickly led me to a pioneer graveyard, and there I found him. The old gentleman had daffodils carved on his gravestone.

My wise old owl.

"Tuck them in, shut them in, and lock the doors behind them!"

Local histories described him as a delightful old Irish man, much beloved by his children, grandchildren and great grandchildren.

I read about festive gatherings in that old cottage, people playing the tin whistle and dancing Irish jigs.

Ah, the music.

I was so sick the whole time we lived there, I had to quit my job. Without the job there was no reason to stay. We found a rental back in town and moved on.

I stopped vomiting immediately.

I took daffodils and whiskey to the grave of my friend, the wise old owl.

Thanks for watching over us, We're safe now.

Years later I met someone living in that house. With no children under the roof, the restless specters of the crossroads seem less drawn to the place. However, he told me the front door still opens in the night, and some-times. they still hear the Irish music, coming from the walls.

A Little Green Man

T hose cheeky kids had moved my plants again. They must have. I'd bought them - shrubs with red flowers - a while back and tucked them between the big potted plants. Just until I had time to plant them out of course. Now they were sitting in the middle of the path.

"Did you kids shift my plants?"

"No. What plants?" Four innocent looking faces.

"The new ones in small plastic pots. Behind the big pots."

"No. We haven't touched them." Four little girls nodded solemnly.

I felt bad for the plants, I knew I should have planted them sooner. They'd been sitting there more than a month. It was my first year working on the farm and I hadn't been prepared for the craziness.

Spring madness.

Hundreds of bawling, mooing, milky-faced babies to feed. Hours bent over the feeder teaching them how to suckle. Hauling buckets of milk and grain. Struggling through rain, wind and mud. I ached in new places every day. I'd watered the new plants from time to time, but I didn't get a minute to transplant them.

The next day when I dragged my tired body home from the calf shed, the plants were out on the path again. I put them back.

"Are you kids trying to be funny? Those plants have moved again!" Four blank stares.

Four sets of shrugged shoulders. I was suspicious though. Cheeky little scamps.

By morning, the pots were back out on the path. When I returned them I noticed that they'd been waiting so long now, their roots were starting to poke out through the holes in the bottom of the pots. I felt a bit guilty. I really must get them planted today.

I didn't.

On my day off, the plants were on the path again. I still thought it must be the kids. Wee devils!

"I don't mind if you want to use them in your games, just put them back afterwards. In case it gets windy." Four little girls looked at me like I was crazy. Crossly, I put the plants back.

We had a big day out and by evening my littlest was tired. She lay down on her bed chatting sleepily to her toys while I cooked dinner. I was heating oil in the pan when I noticed she was quiet. I hoped she wouldn't fall asleep before the food was ready.

"Mummy!" She was still awake. Good.

"Yeah?" I kept chopping onions.

"Mummy, I just saw a little green man. He winked at me!"

"Wait, what?" I put the knife down and poked my head around the door. Her eyes were wide and wondering. Slightly trancelike.

"He was all green and knobbly. Like he was made out of plants."

"Really?"

"He jumped down off the roof and winked at me. Then he jumped back up again."

"Huh? That's interesting..." I smelled the oil smoking and hurried back to the stove, thinking about what she'd seen.

It was still light outside when we finished dinner. A gold-touched spring evening, all sweet air and birdsong. I headed out into the garden and planted the red flowery bushes, giving them a good long watering. They looked much happier.

Perhaps the little green man cared about the feelings of my struggling plants. Maybe he'd moved them to remind me of their distress?

I wasn't sure, but I stopped blaming the kids.

The Haunted Isle

"I grew up here. I lived with ghosts." The man's eyes were bloodshot.

He was probably drunk, stoned, or worse. But that's what trauma does.

His words stayed with me.

As I lived here.

As I worked, travelled, and saw eerie things.

In Tasmania, we know the island is haunted. People are rarely surprised to hear a ghost story. Usually, they have one of their own.

All my short stories are inspired by real uncanny events.

You may doubt that so many creepy things could happen to one person.

But I live in Tasmania.

I live with ghosts.

Custom Made

I don't know which are scarier, the ghosts or the politicians that stay in Hobarts Old Customs House Hotel. Directly across the road from the state government compound, the hotel is the favourite haunt of politicians visiting interstate. And with the sordid history of the building, it's hardly surprising there's a ghost or two as well.

Early Hobart was filled with as many people running rackets as there were opportunities. It was common knowledge that a tunnel ran under the street from the squalid waterfront, directly into the customs building. All manner of goods and contraband were smuggled in. Maybe even people. It was boldly corrupt.

We'd booked at the last minute. There was only one room available. A poky cell half below street level, with an outdated bathroom and all the charm of a broom cupboard. The only window was in the musty bathroom, high up towards the ceiling it let a few drops of natural light trickle into the gloom.

We didn't care. We were just happy to get away from the farm and the family for a few days. We quickly unpacked, showered and dressed for town. Before heading to the bar, I attempted to make one last trip to the bathroom. The door refused to budge.

"What have you done to the door?"

"Nothing, what's wrong?"

"It won't budge. It's locked somehow."

"What the hell?"

We poked and prodded it. Rattled it. Jiggled it and joggled it. Eventually we gave up and headed to the bar. We brainstormed over a couple of drinks about how we might get it open ourselves, without bothering hotel management. We returned, warm with whiskey and full of ideas about credit cards, pens, and pocketknives.

On first touch of the door, it glided open. Unlocked. Not even stiff. Not even squeaky. Weird.

"That's crazy." My partner shook his head.

"It was locked wasn't it?"

"Yes, definitely."

"I'm not going bonkers?"

"Well..." My sweetheart chuckled. "That remains to be seen but the door was definitely locked."

"Ghosts?"

"Maybe. Maybe just a crappy old door."

"But it's perfect now. It doesn't even rattle?"

Whatever. The night was young and Salamaca Place with all its sensuous pleasures called to us, siren of the city. Brightly lit bars and grills spilled joyously onto the street. Fires blazed outside pubs, banishing frosty night air from small glowing circles. Mulled wine, warm spiced cider and hot gin toddies on every corner. We tried one at each bar, then revisited the best for another round.

We ended the night with a chilly wander through St Davids Park, the old cemetery. We meandered through, reading the wall constructed from broken tombstones, searching for my ancestors' names. We marveled at the birthdates of the old folk, stretching back to the 1700's. We poured out a whiskey near the wall for the ancient ones and weaved our unsteady way back to the hotel room.

Nothing was out of the ordinary in the room, not while we stayed up enjoying the last of the night and our momentary freedom from farm life. Not until we decided to sleep.

I snuggled down next to my love, who was already breathing deeply, softly, unconscious.

Bang.

The extractor fan in the bathroom switched itself on. Full force.

Ah balls! I'd never get to sleep with that racket going on. Like a card stuck in a bicycle wheel. I got up and trudged into the bathroom.

I flicked the switch marked, "fan". Nothing changed. The extractor whirred away devilishly. I flicked the other switches on the panel. Just in case.

No joy.

I tried every other switch in the whole damn bathroom. Unceasing whirring and humming blasted out from the fan.

Damn old buildings.

Damn shonky wiring.

Infernal Ghosts.

Whatever!

I was exhausted, it was past midnight — incredibly late for a farmer. I went back to bed and jammed a pillow over my head. I tried to drift off. I floated close to the edge of sleep, but I couldn't sink down.

Whir. Whir. Whir. Buzz.

More than once, I got up irritably to use the bathroom and tried every damn switch in the room again. Each time the result was that the lights came on and off as they were meant to, and the fan cackled noisily in my face. Whir. Whir. Whir. Buzz.

My restless movements woke my partner, and he heard it too. He couldn't get it to shut off either. We slept in fits and starts, the constant droning of the fan pushing its way into our dreams.

Finally, dawn light touched the tiny window in the bathroom. We were both awake already, out of habit. No ill effects from all the mulled wine and hot gin toddies. Morning traffic began to stir. Far away, back on the farm, the roosters would be crowing, proclaiming St Michaels dominion over demons of the night. In that moment the fan switched itself off.

"You are bloody kidding me!" I stomped into the bathroom and tried the switches again. It behaved normally. It turned on and off.

"It ran all bloody night!" I fumed

"I couldn't get it to turn off either."

"It works fine now." I flicked the switch repeatedly to prove my point.

"It could be faulty wiring?"

"Strange how it stopped at dawn though."

"And started the moment we tried to sleep."

"It probably started around midnight come to think of it."

"The light of day chased it back to its grave."

We exchanged glances, a shared shudder.

"I guess we were asking for it, running around in St Davids at night."

"Ghosts?"

"I vote ghosts."

But that's the thing with ghosts and politicians. You never really know the truth.

Madam Rosie Comes Knocking.

I f you dine at Three steps On George, you might be lucky enough to be seated upstairs. From there, you can look down on the bar, on top of which reclines Madam Rosie in all her glory. A larger-than-life antique photograph of the once notorious bordello owner adorns that bar like a languid Venus. She smiles, sweet as a silent film star, stark-naked.

The building was once the gymnasium of the old Launceston Grammar. The sons of

Launceston's elite strained and sweated within its walls. When the school moved to the new site in the 1920's Rosie introduced a very different sweaty activity to the building. Her eight-foot-tall portrait reigned supreme over the main bar, a Goddess in her own domain.

When the doors of the bordello finally closed, the photograph remained with the building. The former house of ill repute was eventually developed into a family restaurant, with wholesome decor, high-chairs and a children's menu. They couldn't have a naked woman towering over the room. Nor could they bear to banish her entirely. So, we always trek up to the mezzanine floor when we stay, to pay our respects and raise a glass to Rosie.

We never expected to encounter her.

I won't claim we hadn't been drinking. We checked into our room and cut loose on the mini bar. A terrible financial decision borne of laziness. We couldn't be bothered looking for a bottle store. Having confessed that, I promise that what happened next was real. There's no amount of alcohol could cause us to imagine it.

Back in those days we used to smoke. We would periodically leave our room and head for the carpark of St Johns Anglican Church adjacent, to indulge our filthy habit.

As midnight approached, we took our drinks outside to have one last smoke. The whole town was quiet. Not a living soul moved around the church or the accommodation. We gazed up at the stars, blowing clouds of smoke into the stillness, stamping our feet to keep warm. We chuckled at the close proximity between Bordello and Church. Scandalous!

When we left, I chose a gap in the hedge, the boundary between piety and lasciviousness, to pour out my offering. Half a can of gin and tonic.

"This one's for you, Rosie old girl."

We didn't pass anyone on the way back to our room. Launceston was unusually quiet. No nightlife or squealing tires. No throbbing engines or sub-woofers. Just the faint hum of a sleeping city. Our footsteps lonely echoes on the walkway.

We slipped inside and began taking our coats off.

Bang! Bang! Bang!

Urgent knocking shook the door in its frame. Brutally loud. Like a police raid at dawn. We stared at each other, speechless in the silence that followed.

There was no question of anyone *living* knocking on our door. It was quiet as the grave out there. As our shivers subsided, we began to giggle nervously.

"I think she wants more gin."

Far away, the town clock tower chimed midnight.

Impeccable timing Madam Rosie.

New Moon Blues

We'd never been to The Blues Festival before.

There was a planning error that year and the event fell on new moon, during wet weather. The site, on the banks of the Forth river was soggy and misty.

Seething with unseen presence.

After dark, we were blind without torches and once drunk, stumbled haplessly toward any light we could see.

I could already feel a thickness in the air, teeming with the dead, long before I saw the first sign of possession.

As alcohol flowed in the bloodstreams of those around me, they began to dip out of themselves, letting someone else take the reins. It didn't matter so much when they were dancing or saying, "I love you." But some turned bitter. Mean. Then they'd snap out of it. With no memory of what was said.

It was chilling to watch their eyes pop back into focus and to hear them deny the words they'd just spoken.

Somehow, we partied through it, forgiving and forgetting. Losing ourselves in the crowd, swept along by the current of chaos.

It was pitch black as we groped our way back into our tent and tried to keep warm in clammy, damp bedding.

I couldn't sleep. Restless shadows swarmed along the riverbank. Not that I could see anything in the solid dark. I felt them. Their whispering rustled like leaves in a breeze, although the air was strangely still.

My partner however, fell unconscious quickly.

I was astonished when he began talking in his sleep.

"I love this town. Always be home to me."

We didn't live nearby.

"No matter what, I'll always come back y'know? I's jus' beautiful. I's born here 'n' I'll die here."

I shivered.

He doesn't talk like that.

"Love it 'ere. Jus' love it."

He groaned and shifted in his sleep, then fell silent.

In the next tent, our mate Al' grunted. He began speaking.

"Love this town ya know? S'always gunna be my home."

I felt cold. More than just the damp chilled me now.

"I'll always come home. Ya know that right? I's jus' beautiful. Born here, 'n' die here. Yeah."

His voice trailed off to a mutter, punctuated by the occasional, "Love it here." Then he too fell silent.

I didn't want to sleep at all now.

I snuggled closer to my man, staring ahead into nothing.

I'd tell them in the morning, over instant coffee.

Maybe, they'd even believe me.

Hidden In the Land

Nymph, nymph, what are your beads?

Green glass, goblin. Why do you stare at them?

Give them me.

No.

Give them me. Give them me.

No.

Then I will howl all night in the reeds,

Lie in the mud and howl for them.

Goblin, why do you love them so?

They are better than stars or water,

Better than voices of winds that sing,

Better than any man's fair daughter,

Your green glass beads on a silver ring.

Hush, I stole them out of the moon.

Give me your beads, I want them.

No.

I will howl in the deep lagoon

For your green glass beads, I love them so.

Give them me. Give them.

No.

Overheard on a Saltmarsh

Harold Monro

The Vampire Trap

It was my favourite time of day. Not when I was dragging my bones out of bed at 3.30, but once we'd thrown back a scalding coffee and headed into the dark.

I'd wrap my arms tightly around my husband Paul, as the farm bike roared to life. I laid my cold cheek against the heat of his back and watched the last shadows of night speed by. The pristine hours before dawn felt sacred; a church for the music of night-birds with a vaulted ceiling of stars. If it rained, I pressed my face into his coat, letting his broad shoulders shield me. Too soon the engine shut off and I'd have to wrench myself away from him, bracing myself for a long shift milking.

Normally I'd set up the dairy while he headed out to get the cows. However, on this particular morning, as I prepared to hook up the vat, the digital display flashed angrily.

"Hey!" I called urgently to Paul before he could roar off into the night. "There's an error code. Can you take a look?"

As Paul puzzled over the screen, tapping buttons, I snaked my arm around the door groping for the light-switch. When I found it, there was no bright flash of cold halogen. Instead, a dull yellowish glow slowly emerged from each light fitting, then faded again, fluctuating with an eerie rhythm.

"I've never seen that before." Paul sounded grim. "I'll have to call someone. We can't milk with the power on the fritz."

"Do you think it could be because of what happened yesterday?"

"I hope not. I told those bloody contractors to mind out for the graves."

Old Mr. Peterson from over the road had called the day before, highly agitated. As soon the call finished, Paul leapt on the bike and raced to other side of the farm with reckless speed, but it was too late. The contractors, clearing away the old pig pen, had demolished the graves of the Wells family with it.

"I bloody told them last week." Paul fumed. "They knew the graves were there. Damn contractors, arrogant pricks!"

We had a personal stake in the protection of those graves. It wasn't purely out of respect for community heritage. It was also self-preservation. The angry spirit of Esther Wells had never rested peacefully, preferring to torment the living and lure pets out onto the road in front of trucks. She'd plagued me when I first came to the farm.

In those early days I didn't even know the graves existed. I threw myself headlong into the adventure of farm life. It was exhilarating after years of being a stay-at-home mother, being outside in the fresh countryside.

I watched great flocks of ravens grow fat on left over milk, grain and carrion; I saw hares, wallabies, possums and cockatoos. A lone hawk often circled lazily above. The land herself had a thousand moods and even when it turned fierce, spectacular double rainbows arced across the sky amid the tempest.

I loved feeding the calves. The mornings were frosty; hollows of daisies edged in crispy white lined the laneways as I sped by on the farm bike. Sweet, wet-nosed babies, sucked my fingers, clambering all over me as I arrived in the morning. As they grew older, I'd tow a mobile feeder out to the pasture for them, waiting as each mob sucked and gurgled, leaving a ring of cappuccino froth on the ground when the feeder was towed away.

It was only when I was in the top paddock, waiting for the calves to drink, that I felt miserable. A maudlin chill would wash over me. Tears would spill down my cheeks before I even knew why I was sad. *It all just felt so unfair.* Every shitty circumstance I'd ever faced came swirling back to me in a dark miasma. A black cloak settled over my shoulders, damp with self-pity. I'd slump the seat of the farm bike and cry until the calves were finished.

As I towed the feeder back to the dairy to refill, I felt better. By the time I got home I'd forget all about it. Until I noticed the pattern. Top paddock. Every damn time.

It was at the Christmas party I found out about the graves.

Somehow, between cans of pre-mixed whiskey and barbequed steak people began sharing ghost stories.

"There's something kind *off* about the top paddock." I was tentative, in case they laughed me down.

"Well, that's close to the graves." A farm-hand nodded thoughtfully. "Makes sense"

"What graves?"

"They're on the other side of the stock yards. Down by the old piggery. You'd probably have to dig around to find them under all the weeds."

My interest was piqued. I soon found the graves. Smothered by long grass, the delicate fence surrounding them butted right up to the old pig pen. Piles of rusting tin stacked up on one side and an ancient effluent drain curved round the other. Tangled blackberry scratched my legs as I watched carefully for snakes. The graves were surprisingly substantial. A concrete top and matching plaques; Mother Dearest, Father Dearest. Harry and Esther Wells. His and hers, matching.

I counted the dates. Poor Esther, only 52. Harry had outlived her by years. A thrill of excitement stirred in my belly. *I'll make friends with them.* I had very little experience with the dead back then. It didn't occur to me that a ghost who makes you cry might not make a good friend.

I visited and left small gifts on the graves periodically. I tidied up the weeds and rubbish. My good deeds didn't go unpunished.

Bad things began to happen. Sad feelings overwhelmed me most days, dropping out of nowhere. The children couldn't sleep. The oldest dreamed there were knives all over the floor, pointing upwards, cutting her feet. The little one complained about a pair of disembodied blue eyes hanging in space, watching her. The middle child dreamed that a lady in a long dress touched the vine growing over our house, making it wither and die.

Our cats were both run over. We got another cat, but he vanished too. Our bunnies died and our dog got sick.

Then one day I saw her.

I was working near the graves. It was a perfect, sunny afternoon, no hint of precipitation. Yet as I watched, a misty shape curled like smoke rising from a chimney, above the tombstones. The spectral cloud glided purposefully toward me then vanished leaving a horrible feeling in its wake. I felt sick. A sense of loathing washed over my whole body.

She *hated* me. *She* was a good Christian woman. I drank and smoked and swore. I dabbled with the occult. *Shameful*. I wanted to vomit as I backed away towards the bike, tearing home across the paddocks at top speed.

I had to face the truth. I'd invited a malevolent entity into my home. She was dangerous. She was hurting my family.

Shit.

I knew what I had to do.

I gathered materials for a spirit trap. Some people call them vampire traps. Where modern media makes a clear distinction between ghosts and vampires, folk magic doesn't.

To the old people, a vampire was a particularly solid revenant with a fondness for blood. All the dead who roamed with malefic intent were all regarded as vampiric. Attracted to shiny things, particularly coins, they're compelled to count tiny objects such as grains of rice. They can become tangled in string and be pierced by nails.

You *could* stake the grave with rosewood stakes, but the thick concrete grave topper negated that option for me.

I filled the biggest jar I could find with rice, hiding a nest of tangled thread in the centre, laced with nails. I pushed coins into the jar around the outer edges where they'd be visible. Then I placed the jar on the grave at sunset. When dawn broke the following day, I retrieved the jar and drove hours until I reached a particularly lonely crossroads. I buried it there and hurried away, making sure I never looked back.

It was quiet after that. My moods evened out, the children slept peacefully, and our pets thrived. We hadn't experienced a sinister moment in three years, but now we were worried. Our anxiety increased as the day went on and Paul found more problems on the farm. The motors on the pivot irrigators had burned out. The electric fencing units were fried. Even the portable circuit breakers, designed to prevent any surges, had melted. I shuddered. Esther was *raging*.

I had to let her know it wasn't our fault, hopefully then she wouldn't come after us. Maybe if she understood it was the owner of the farm who'd authorized the demolition, she'd focus her fury elsewhere? Optimistically I wrote her a little note and burned it, burying the ashes with some flowers and a few coins. I suppose I'd forgotten the strength of her hatred.

The next morning, the power had been fixed, and as usual, I set up the dairy. I moved around the platform lifting sets of cups off jetters and pressing buttons on cup-removing units to raise them. As I circled the platform, I began to feel sad. I was so tired, it was so early. It wasn't even fair I had to work so hard. Why had I *even* married a farmer? Dark thoughts swirled thick and fast around me when I was distracted by a sudden movement. On the other side of the platform, cups I'd already set up began falling back down.

Godssakes. I muttered under my breath. Now I'd have to do them all again. I stopped, struck by a swift realization. I knew this dank feeling. It wasn't mine. That *bitch* was following me around the dairy, undoing my work, pouring *her* misery all over me like poison.

I knew what I had to do.

There was a large, dead rose bush in the garden. After milking I carefully I fashioned six sharp stakes from the old bush. Might as well stake Harry too, just to be thorough. I went into town and bought a whole sack of rice, then I rode the farm bike to the other side of the farm.

There was only a smooth dark scar in the pasture to show where the pig pen, the graves, had ever been. I knew every curve of that land though. I knew the exact spot, the soft slope of the hillock where they rested. My feet easily returned to where I'd stood to offer little gifts to her, years ago, when I thought we could be friends.

I scattered the rice thickly in a huge equal armed cross covering both graves. Then I got down on my knees in the dirt and hammered. One stake for the head, one for the heart and one for the feet. His and hers, matching.

I stood back and admired my handiwork.

Goodbye Esther Wells.

Maybe I'll see you in hell.

Holding The Town Together

The spectral ladies of the Country Women's Association pressed around me in the musty, unlit room. Pillbox hats perched on tightly curled grey hair. A gaggle of white Sunday gloves and horn-rimmed spectacles hemming me in on all sides.

"But you are connected to this town." They whispered insistently. *"You are."*

"I'm not!" I backed away from their colourless faces. "I'm not related to *anyone* in Tasmania."

"*You are.*" They nodded in unison. "*You're connected to the Hollington family.*"

"I'm not though, am I?"

I spoke the last words aloud to an empty room, coldly awake now. Pulling my blankets tighter around me, I reflected on the strange dream. The building was familiar. I'd spent countless hours in our tiny local museum. I pictured it, dark and empty overnight, the artifacts of a rural community sleeping in the shadows.

It couldn't be true, could it? Everything I knew about my family history belonged in New Zealand. Sure, there were gaps if you went back far enough, but this? No doubt, just wishful thinking.

I was desperate to truly connect with the town. That was the first reason I'd volunteered.

In a place run on the strength of surnames, blood ties and shared history, I was a newcomer. A stranger from a whole different country. Having failed to marry into any of the old families, I was marked forever as an outsider. I knew if I reached down into the graves of the early settlers, I could grasp hold of the roots of the community. From there, maybe I could graft myself onto the tree.

I also hungered to find the truth; did I have the second sight or was I insane? My dreams were like a hectic magic lantern show of events from other people's lives. Even awake, when I handled certain objects, fleeting visions danced across my mind. Skidding in old boots on a frozen pond. Pouring fragrant raspberry filling into pies. The bright splash of flowers on a tiny grave. A house with white weatherboards that will *always* be home.

Some nights the stories were dark, violent, full of gristle and pain.

I gained access to the archives; old newspapers, letters and photographs. Often enough, I found my stories. Eerie coincidences of time and place that matched my dreams. Other secrets remained buried, but I'd come to trust they were real moments, locked in the land, whispering their truth for anyone who could hear.

Lastly, I simply enjoyed being there. The old building had a sentimental smell, like a favourite book. Stories folded neatly into corners, atop shelves that once held linen and soap, haberdashery and household goods. Creaking boards divided the old parts of the building from the even older parts. The shop, the post office, the cottage.

Nothing spooky ever happened, but there was a presence. Not the chilly sensation of being watched, but the warmer feeling of being watched *over*. It seemed to me, that if it was haunted, it was by the past committee members of the Country Women's Association.

Wearing pill-box hats to meetings and white gloves to cover their work-worn hands. Throwing home-made floral house coats over black dresses and serving afternoon tea at a wake. Arranging perfect sponge cakes and delicately crocheted doilies for charity stalls before returning home to early morning starts and ceaseless toil on the farm.

Women who quietly held the town together, their stories written in tiny, neat little stitches and spidery notes scribbled in the margins of recipe books. They knew everyone in our tiny community, had a remedy for every ill, an adage for every situation.

I felt them listening, while I chatted the mornings away with Lois, the museum co-ordinator. Our conversations roamed freely between the past and the present but always stayed firmly within the town boundaries. Lois was woven into fabric of the place from birth, steeped in it. She loved it as one loves a flawed family member, with a mixture of loyalty and exasperation. I loved it like a high school crush, hoping it might one day love me back.

One morning I sorted books in the read-ing room, while Lois clicked quietly on her keyboard next door. I wondered about my latest odd dream. *Surely not?* It was easier to trust stories about other people's lives. I had too much interest in belonging to be impar-tial. *Not all dreams are psychic visions.* Still, it wouldn't hurt to check.

There was a stack of family histories on one of the shelves. The Hollington book was a particularly thick volume. Complete family trees branched out in every direction, a thick forest of names and dates. I ran my finger quickly down each list, reading hundreds of names. I flicked through page after page. Then my finger stopped. One of the Hollington boys had married a girl whose surname jumped off the page at me. My grandmother's maiden name. Not a common name either. I had never actually met a living person whose surname was Loring.

"Lois!" I rushed into the next room. "Do we have Lorings around here?" Lois looked up from her keyboard.

"Yes, for sure, at least, there's quite a few of them further up the coast."

"That's my grandmother's maiden name. Maybe I'm related?"

"Oooooh." A three-second sound of genuine interest. "Maybe. Why don't you get on the Tasmanian names index and have a look?"

The name Loring produced quite a few results from the early era of Tasmania. All the way back to when we were Van Diemen's Land. As I scrolled through, one birth record from Hobart stood out. It was familiar. My grandmother's grandfather, who'd come out to New Zealand to fight in our civil war. I'd always believed he'd come from England.

A common first name though. There could be plenty of Samuel Lorings worldwide. I'd have to dig deeper.I ordered records from the New Zealand registrar of births, deaths and marriages.

I felt antsy, like a kid who'd entered a competition, excited to check the mailbox every day.

Would it change things if I had blood here? Was that why this isolated rural community felt strangely like home, right from the start? On the other hand, if I wasn't connected, where did that leave me? An outsider who had weird dreams and 'saw things' sometimes.

It took two weeks to arrive. I tore it open immediately, sitting in the car on our dusty driveway. I finally had my answer. It *was* my ancestor who was born in Hobart, all those years ago. The other Lorings were his brothers, sisters, uncles, aunties and cousins. Tracing branches all the way out to the twigs I was related to hundreds of people all over Tasmania, with many different surnames. Intricately connected to the whole island, and certainly to the tiny corner I lived in.

I sighed, staring out the window. Connected by blood, surname and shared history after all. Who would have guessed?

Mind you, those ghostly ladies of the Country Women's Association knew all along. They always do. They know everyone in our tiny community, have a remedy for every ill, an adage for every situation.

They hold the town together.

Next time they hold a committee meeting in my dreams, I'll trust their advice.

Old Farmer and the Tithe to Hell

C rap. Someone had left a gate open.

Two gates.

Shit.

The cows bolted down the laneway, their eyes lighting up as they spied lush grass, straight ahead. The paddock they were meant to go into, next to it, was already half grazed. Unappealing.

There was no way I'd get on the other side of them now, even on the quad. I could only watch helplessly as the mob kicked up their heels, charging hungrily toward their grazing.

It was a whole extra job now. I'd have to go push them off that good grass after milking and put them in the right paddock.

They wouldn't want to move.

It was sure to be a bastard of a job, and I'd yell myself hoarse by the time I got it done.

As the first cow made it to the open gateway, they all suddenly baulked. Dozens of hooves, screeched to a halt, mid gallop, making dust puff up around them.

As one, they turned obediently away from the smorgasbord of greenery in front of them. Meekly, the whole mob filed around the corner into the correct paddock. All I had to do was follow up with the quad and latch the gate.

As I hooked handles back into powered loops, I shook my head, puzzled. Cows don't turn corners. Not if they can help it. The only thing that could have stopped them charging into that fresh paddock, barring a gate, would be if someone stood in the gap waving their arms wildly...

Thanks, Old farmer.

I smiled into the empty space around me. It must have been *him*.

It wasn't the first time we'd had an unseen helper, and it wouldn't be the last.

One afternoon my son was milking by himself in the rotary dairy. It was a tough season and the cows were hungry. Unsatisfied with their rations of grain, the bolshy girls charged back onto the platform after being milked, hoping for another feed on the milking merry-go-round.

It was frustrating. The poor lad had to stop the platform and run up there to shoo them out repeatedly. Morning milking, we had a second person at cups-off, spraying teats and making the cows flow off the platform smoothly. In the afternoons however, we had the automatic teat sprayer. Good for soaking udders in iodine, hopeless for moving stubborn cattle.

My son became increasingly upset. For every set of cups he put on a cow, he had to stop everything, run up a set of steps, dart into the bails, wave and flap and chase the cow far enough down the raceway to keep her going.

Sometimes they turned back anyway.

Especially the heifers. It was ridiculous. He felt like he was going to be there until midnight, as every single damn cow refused to move.

He reached his breaking point. Tears welled up in his eyes.

If ONE more cow refuses to get off, I'm going to totally lose it.

Dwelling on his sorrow for a moment, he tranced out, wrapped in his thoughts. He put on three sets of cups without thinking, then remembered to check the platform.

He glanced up just in time.

A sly cow had edged up, trying to slip back on. Before he could even pull the stop-cord, she spooked dramatically. At nothing. Along with the other three cows, some stalling in their bails rather than backing out, others hovering, she burst backward. They scudded off the rotary, flying down the raceway as if the Devil himself were chasing them.

My son was astonished. There was nothing he could see that could have startled those cows. Even if there had been, a hungry cow is stubborn, impervious to most things.

I think I just met Old Farmer. He smiled to himself then, and although the rest of the milking wasn't perfect, his heart lifted. After all, *someone* cared.

Cared enough to cross the great divide, just to chase cows.

It's quiet for me now, living in town. My house isn't haunted, and if the neighbours' houses are, the spectres mind their own business.

It was different on the farm.

In the hush of the land, the otherworld was loud. More than one paddock held old graves that were still visible, although during our time, some were demolished.

Other secrets in the land had long gone under, but if you asked the oldest folk, they'd point to a bare hill and tell you about the houses, the school, the church that once stood there.

The farm constantly devoured pristine bushland, more each year. There was a sense of anger in the disturbed soil at the junction between wild and newly cleared land. As trees were destroyed, noisy machinery violently pushed back the habitats of the swift parrot, the wedge tailed eagle, devils and quolls.

Shrinking the kingdom of those uncanny *other* beings, whose allegiance is not to us.

Folklore has always been concerned with hedges, with charms and wards to keep *them* out. Where farm meets forest or lonely roads stray into the woods; here two worlds overlap. Denizens of that vast *other* might easily cross over.

The old country folk knew it. With one eye on the weather and the evergreen possibility of encountering a snake or being trampled by cattle, the fortunes of country people are at natures mercy. Our ancestor's magic was rural. Witches stole butterfat or soured the milk. Fair folk rode horses to exhaustion in the night, or made mischief for the farmer, maybe even lured his fine strong sons away to Faerie forever.

After all, there's always a nagging sense of debt. The tithe to hell. Our uneasy knowledge that those we continually take from, as we hack at their world to expand our own, might demand something back.

There were too many eerie experiences, living on the edge of the hedge, to give each one a story. Many were fleeting moments, or strange sightings with no explanation, leaving only a question mark in my mind.

The man I glimpsed in a checked shirt, in broad daylight, gone a moment later. Distant voices, right on the edge of hearing. Or a loud shout, from an empty hillside, calling my name.

Early one morning I watched in fascination as a solid black shadow played around our table legs for several minutes. More than once, I felt my husband climb into bed and put his arms around me, only to realise, he wasn't there.

The sight isn't strictly visual. I heard, felt and dreamed eerie things.

In sleep I talked to Old Farmer, proudly showing me his dairy. A visiting friend dreamed she had a conversation with him in our bathroom. We all dreamed about the little girl and the eighteen-year-old boy, so proud to show us around the farm. It was years before we found out they were siblings who'd died there.

Then there was the unsettling feeling, when working alone close to the bush-line, of being watched by unseen eyes. Eyes that have never been human.

In my bed in town, I hear cars revving their engines instead. Light from other homes pushes through the gaps in the curtains. The train whistle blows. Yet somehow, it's too quiet.

My dreams feel dull, ordinary. A bunch of clatter and chatter with no real meaning. Except when they pull me back in time, and I fly once more over that landscape. Soaring above the hills, whose every curve I know. Down below, I spy a tumbled down old dairy.

Old farmer is bringing in his cows, forever, while a little girl and her older brother watch. The land is filled with sound and movement. Animal, human and *other*.

Part of me is there forever too, locked in the dreaming of the land, whose butterfat *I* have skimmed.

Paying my tithe.

Why did They bring me here to make me
      Not quite bad and not quite good,
      Why, unless They're wicked, do They want, in spite, to take me
      Back to their wet, wild wood ?
      Now, every night I shall see the windows shin-
ing,
      The gold lamp's glow, and the fire's red
gleam,
      While the best of us are twining twigs and the
rest of us are whining
      In the hollow by the stream.
      Black and chill are Their nights on the wold;

And They live so long and They feel no pain:
I shall grow up, but never grow old,
I shall always, always be very cold,
I shall never come back again !

The Changeling
Charlotte Mew
1869 –1928

Authors Note

If you enjoyed this creepy chocolate box of offerings, you might also enjoy my haunted romance, Heart Of A Warrior available in paperback and eBook from all the usual places.

I love hearing from my readers, so don't be shy to pop into my socials!

Vanessa Amohia Jones on Facebook and Vanessa_Amohia_Jones on Instagram.

9 781763 623224